MW01071526

For Loretta

The illustrations in this book were created digitally using an iPad Pro and Procreate.

Cataloging-in-Publication Data has been applied for and
may be obtained from the Library of Congress.

ISBN 978-1-4197-5392-3

Book design by Jade Rector

Published in 2022 by Abrams Books for Young Readers, an imprint of ABRAMS.

Printed and bound in China
10 9 8 7 6 5 4 3 2 1

Abrams Books for Young Readers are available at special discounts
when purchased in quantity for premiums and promotions as well as fundraising
or educational use. Special editions can also be created to specification.
For details, contact specialsales@abramsbooks.com or the address below.

Abrams® is a registered trademark of Harry N. Abrams, Inc.

ABRAMS The Art of Books
195 Broadway, New York, NY 10007
abramsbooks.com

Murray Christmas

by E. G. Keller

Abrams Books for Young Readers ✻ New York

Murray was a very good boy.
He loved his humans.
He loved his home.

And he *really* loved his job:

He took his job seriously.

Very seriously.

Nothing would come between him and the humans he loved.

One day, he was making his rounds
when the humans did the most peculiar thing:

They planted a tree
in the living room.

CHRISTMAS
STUFF

Murray was troubled by how quickly his home changed after that. The house was no longer safe! Threats lurked *everywhere*.

He **SNATCHED** a flashy snake!

He **CHOMPED** on the army of tiny (admittedly tasty) people!

He **GRRRRRR**ed at the smelly sticks.

He **PUUUUUULLLLLED** at the laundry that was wrongly hung on the fireplace.

He **HARROOOOOOOO**ed to drown out
the terrible sounds coming from the front stoop.

But Murray's home wasn't the only thing that had changed.

And a peculiar person began
popping up everywhere.

Who *was* this guy?
Murray's humans seemed to love him.

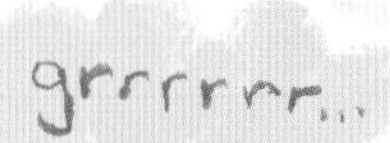

But Murray wasn't impressed.

On a snowy night, after one last patrol of the house . . .

creak

Dear Santa,

HIM!

THE **MESS!**

What would happen when
everyone woke up tomorrow?

This wouldn't do at all!

Though he couldn't understand why this odd fellow
didn't simply use the front door like everyone else . . .

. . . Murray began to see why everyone liked him so much.

And the next morning . . .

. . . there was even a gift for Murray.

VERY HELPFUL
DOG